SONG OF
Moon Pony

Hannah, Mary Jane,
Natalie, & Lily Clark:
wonder & beauty
are all
around! (look!)
— Robby McMurtry

written and illustrated by

Robby McMurtry

EAKIN PRESS · Austin, Texas

This first one is for Lesa.

FIRST EDITION
Copyright © 2003
By Robby McMurtry
Published in the United States of America
By Eakin Press
A Division of Sunbelt Media, Inc.
P.O. Drawer 90159 ⬠ Austin, Texas 78709-0159
email: sales@eakinpress.com
💻 website: www.eakinpress.com 💻
ALL RIGHTS RESERVED.

1 2 3 4 5 6 7 8 9
1-57168-740-8
Library of Congress Control Number: 2002156381

All these things happened long, long ago, before the People had many
ponies, when the buffalo grazed over the prairie in numbers beyond counting,
in a time when the white man and the black man were only stories told and
hardly believed. The People wandered up and down the plains,
always hunting for meat for their kettles
and hides for their clothing and tepees.
In those times things happened—
things we can hardly imagine.

The night was very dark. Black snow clouds covered the sky. There was no moon. There were no stars. Icy winds howled and brought snow.

The People's tepees glowed brightly in the blizzard. The fires were stoked high against the chill.

It was the time of the Hungry Moon. And in the tepee of Antelope Woman, a boy-child was born.

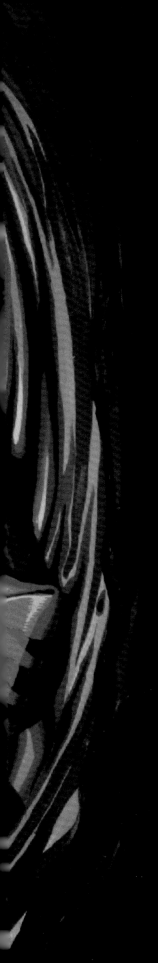

Antelope Woman's sister was there with her, and she wrapped the boy-child in warm furs. The sister said, "He is a strong boy-child, but something is wrong with his face."

Antelope Woman held him closer to the fire and looked. She saw that one eye was higher than the other, and his little nose was crooked. His mouth was pushed over to the side of his face.

Antelope Woman spoke to her baby. "The People will call him Twisted Face. But I give you a secret name. Your secret name is Song Maker. We will never tell your secret name, but someday all the People will know it." Then she sang to him:

"The North Wind is bitter,
Don't cry, don't cry.
Wolf is hungry,
But our fire is warm."

In time, the ice and snow were gone, and the Hungry Moon became the Green Grass Moon. The rivers flowed deep and wide. The buffalo returned. Twisted Face grew.

Twisted Face had no father. His father had been killed in war with the Dog Eaters, the enemies of the People. But he had many uncles, and they taught him to use the bow. They taught him to ride the ponies, and they taught him how to watch for sign on the earth and in the sky.

Buffalo Chief was the leader of the People. He said when it was time to move the camp. He said when the men should hunt the buffalo, and when they should make war on the Dog Eaters. The People followed him because they respected him.

When the leaves began to fall, when the grasses turned yellow, a girl-child was born in Buffalo Chief's tepee. Buffalo Chief looked at her, and he saw how beautiful she was. He told all the People she would be called Moon Pony. He talked to her and said, "Your black eyes will see only the wind and the spirits. You will see into the hearts of men, but you will never see the waking world."

Moon Pony was blind.

Buffalo Chief took his little daughter to the top of a small mountain. He held her high above his head and called, "Eagle!"

Eagle circled in the sky above them. Buffalo Chief shouted to him, "Eagle, this child is mine! She is a part of me, and I love her, but she is blind. You have the sharpest eyes in this world, and you can give her eyes to see the waking world. If you give her sight when she is ready to become a wife, she will be your wife!"

Eagle called back with a scream, and the wind carried him away.

The Moon of the Wild Goose was the time of the great hunt, and the People pulled down their tepees and followed the great herds. Men on ponies chased the buffalo and brought them down with bow and arrow. Women cut the meat into strips and hung it to dry in the sun, to be ready for the Hungry Moon. Everyone ate, and then they ate again.

Twisted Face grew tall and strong. He had many friends. They swam in the streams together and raced their ponies over the prairies. Brown Boy was his best friend. Sometimes they hunted rabbits together.

oon Pony grew also. She was the most beautiful girl the People had ever seen. She could not see, but she listened to the earth as it breathed beneath her. The wind told her its secrets, and she understood the language of the waterbirds. Her friend Jumping Girl led her to the banks of the river, and they talked while the waters rolled by.

As one moon followed another, all the children grew into young men and women. Twisted Face and Brown Boy, Moon Pony and Jumping Girl, and the others helped to care for the little children. They taught them the things they had already learned.

Another moon. Twisted Face and Brown Boy went out to the high places and asked the Creator to bless them. They rode with the men, chasing the buffalo and capturing the wild ponies. They scouted, always on the lookout for the Dog Eaters.

When the young women went out to dig for roots, or when they gathered wood, Moon Pony always stood nearby, listening. She knew where Rattlesnake slept, and Blackbird told her when Grizzly was coming.

Another moon, and another. Young men sat outside the tepees, singing love songs in the night, and the young women came out to sit with them or walk under the stars.

Twisted Face sat outside Jumping Girl's tepee and sang to her. Jumping Girl liked the young man, but she did not come out to sit or walk with him, because he was Twisted Face.

He tried to talk with other young women. All of them knew he had a good heart, but none would sit with him, because he was Twisted Face.

Twisted Face became a great hunter. He brought meat to his mother, Antelope Woman, and to the old people. He also became a fierce warrior. The Dog Eaters feared him, because he was Twisted Face, and he took their ponies.

One afternoon, as he returned from another hunt, he saw Moon Pony sitting alone on a prairie covered with flowers, red and blue. She was facing toward the mountains, and she sang:

"*He must see my footprints;*
When will my husband come?
He knows I am here;
When will my husband come?"

*T*wisted Face rode toward her and got off his pony.

"Hello, Twisted Face," Moon Pony said.

"How did you know it was me?" Twisted Face asked.

Moon Pony smiled. "Maybe the grasses told me. Sit with
me for a while, Twisted Face. Tell me about the waking world."

He looked at her beautiful face for a moment and said,
"Today, the world is all red and blue flowers."

"I can smell the flowers," said Moon Pony, "but red and blue are
things I don't understand. Tell me more."

"High above us," he told her, "there are clouds in the sky."

Moon Pony turned her face upward. "I know the sky, because
the wind lives there, and I can feel the wind and sun on my face.
I know the clouds send the rain, but I cannot imagine clouds.
If I could touch the clouds, maybe I would understand them."

"No man can touch the clouds. No man can
understand them," said Twisted Face. "The Creator
sends them on the wind, and we can only look
at them and wonder."

*M*oon Pony held her face toward the sky, and Twisted Face looked into her beautiful dark eyes. "Tell me about our People," she said.

"Some of the People are tall, some are short. Some of them are brave, and others are afraid of shadows. Some of them are fat . . ."

Moon Pony laughed. "Yes, I know these things. Tell me things I do not know."

Twisted Face closed his eyes and thought about the People.

"Brown Boy has a little scar on his chin from falling off his pony. Jumping Girl smiles all the time, all day long."

"Good!" Moon Pony said. "Tell me more!"

"My mother, Antelope Woman, likes to paint little circles on her cheeks," Twisted Face said, "and your mother likes to paint the part in her hair. Your father, Buffalo Chief, always braids his pony's tail."

"Yes! Keep talking!"

"Big Knife is very handsome, and the girls are always looking at him," said Twisted Face, "but I am very ugly, and the girls turn away from me."

"Handsome . . . Ugly . . ." said Moon Pony. "I hear these words, but I do not understand what they mean."

"They are the ways a man can look. They are what a man is. Handsome. Ugly. Or in-between."

"I cannot look at a man, so I don't know about handsome or ugly," Moon Pony said.

"The People say you can see into men's hearts," Twisted Face told her.

"Yes, I can see into their hearts, and sometimes I do not like the things I see there," she answered. "I see into your heart, Twisted Face. I see that you have a brave and true heart, a good heart."

Twisted Face and Moon Pony sat and talked until the sun began to go down, and they walked back to the camp of their People.

The days grew longer, and the nights were warm. One morning, Twisted Face went to the tepee of Buffalo Chief.

"Sit down, my friend," said Buffalo Chief. He lit his pipe and passed it to Twisted Face, and they smoked without talking.

When they were done, Buffalo Chief waited politely for his visitor to speak. Twisted Face said, "I am alone in the world, Buffalo Chief."

"You are not alone," Buffalo Chief answered. "You have your mother. You have all our People."

"My mother is old, and someday she will pass into the spirit world," said Twisted Face. "No young women will walk or sit with me, because I am Twisted Face." Buffalo Chief didn't answer, and Twisted Face went on. "Only your daughter, Moon Pony, knows my true heart. I come today to ask you to let me take her for my wife."

"You know that I promised Eagle she would be his wife someday," said Buffalo Chief. "All the People know this."

"Then I will go to Eagle, and I will ask him to release her from this promise."

"Eagle will never do that, my friend," said Buffalo Chief. "He will take her for his wife, and he will give her eyes to see the waking world."

Twisted Face stood up. "I will give him many, many ponies," he said, and he turned to leave.

Buffalo Chief called after him,

What use are ponies to Eagle?"

*T*wisted Face visited with the old men, and they told him Eagle lived somewhere in the mountains. No man knew where Eagle slept, though.

Twisted Face rode out on his best pony. He rode west, toward the distant mountains.

When he passed through the country of the Dog Eaters, he slept during the day and traveled at night, under the stars.

The land was drier now, and there was very little grass. Then, there was no grass at all, only dust and rocks. His pony was weak, so Twisted Face let him go and sent him back to the camp.

There were no rivers. There was no water anywhere, but Twisted Face walked on, and he became weaker. He could see the mountains now, but they were still far, far away.

His eyes grew dim, his tongue swelled with thirst, and his strength left him. Twisted Face lay down to die.

Back in the camp, young boys played war and hunting games, and they pretended to be Twisted Face. Brown Boy sat on a little hill nearby and waited for his friend to return. Antelope Woman prayed and asked the Creator to protect her son.

When Twisted Face's pony came back, the People said he must have gone on to the spirit world, but Moon Pony stood on the prairie at sunset and sang:

"His heart is brave.
He will return.
His heart is true.
He will return."

As Twisted Face lay on the hard, dry earth, he felt his spirit begin to go out of him, and he heard a tiny voice say, "I am medicine." He opened his eyes. There, just beside his face, a little cactus grew, and he heard the little voice again. "I am medicine."

His arms were weak and his fingers were stiff, but Twisted Face pulled the little cactus out of the ground. It was not like any cactus he had ever seen. It was very, very small, and it had no thorns. The cactus spoke to him again. "I am medicine."

Twisted Face put the cactus into his mouth and began to chew. It was very bitter, but the moisture inside it seeped into his mouth and strength flowed into his blood.

Weakly, he got to his feet and walked on, toward the mountains. Now and then, he found more cactus, and ate them, and they made him stronger and stronger. When he came to the foothills below the mountains, the sun was going down. Twisted Face slept.

$\mathcal{I}$n the dawn, he began the long climb, up and up and up, higher and higher, over giant boulders and along dizzy cliffs. The air was thin and cold where the snows never melted, where the big winds always blew.

Twisted Face climbed all day, until he reached the place where there was nothing more to climb. He was on the top of all the world, and to the west he could see the edge of it, where the sun slept. Behind him, he saw the dry lands and the prairies beyond them. Far, far away, he could see a tiny silver river.

Twisted Face shouted into the wind, "Eagle!" He held his arms high and shouted again, "Eagle!"

The great bird dropped from the sky and stood on a rock nearby. His wings were spread wide, and he threw a giant shadow across the young man.

"My name is Twisted Face. I have come from far away to speak to you."

"I know who you are—Twisted Face, the great hunter and warrior. I've watched you many times," Eagle said, "and I know why you've come."

"No other young woman will look at me, because I am Twisted Face."

Eagle's yellow eyes flashed, and he said, "You cannot have Moon Pony. She is promised to me. I will give her eyes."

*T*wisted Face said, "I will give you many, many ponies. A hundred!"

"I have no use for ponies," Eagle said. "They are slow. They cannot even fly."

Twisted Face said, "I will bring you fresh meat every day."

"I am the greatest hunter in this world, in the sky, everywhere," said Eagle, and he turned away and spread his wings again.

Twisted Face hung his head. He had nothing more to offer, and Moon Pony would never belong to him. He turned to begin the long walk back to the People.

"Wait," Eagle said. "I cannot let you have Moon Pony, but I give you this," and he pulled a flute from under his wing. Twisted Face had never seen a flute before, and he had no word for it. "I know your true name," said Eagle. "When you use this, all the People will know it."

Twisted Face took the strange gift, and he went down the mountain. As he walked, he gathered the little cactuses. He would take this new medicine back to the People. Whenever he rested, he studied the flute. He looked through it, and he listened to it, and he smelled it. He blew into it, and a strange, beautiful sound floated out! He found that he could change the sound when he put his fingers over the little holes, and he found that he could make the sounds sing.

After a long time, he stood on a hill and saw the camp of his People below. He saw Moon Pony, sitting in the grass and singing.

A shadow passed quickly over Twisted Face, and he looked up to see Eagle riding the wind. Eagle turned and circled high above the camp, and all the People watched. Eagle swooped lower, circling again, and then flew into the camp. He brushed some of the People with his great wings and turned to fly around Moon Pony.

One circle, and she stood up, still singing. Two circles, and Eagle's wings swept the earth, throwing up dust. Three, and Moon Pony opened her arms and began to spin with Eagle. Four. The dust was a whirlwind now, as Moon Pony's arms were wings, and her eyes saw the world below. She and Eagle passed through the clouds and were gone.

Twisted Face tried to forget Moon Pony. He began making songs with his gift. The People heard, and they went out to him. Men touched their ears and listened. Children held up their hands to capture the sounds. All the young women stood close to him and wondered at the beautiful songs he made, and the songs made him beautiful.

He was no longer Twisted Face.

His name was Song Maker.

About the Author

ROBBY MCMURTRY is of Scotch-Irish, Cajun, and Comanche descent. He lives near Okmulgee, Oklahoma, with his wife Lesa, grandson Jet, and assorted dogs and horses. He says he has a thousand stories.